WHO'S INVITED?

Sun

I'm a massive, glowing ball of hydrogen and helium gases. A star! Some call me ordinary, since there are billions like me in the Milky Way galaxy. But it's my gravity that draws in the family of planets, moons, asteroids, and comets that makes up our solar system. We started 4.6 billion years ago as a giant swirling cloud of gas and dust particles. First, the gravity at the center pulled in most of the cloud, and it collapsed to form me—Sun! Then other debris collided and congealed into larger bodies that became the planets. What a chaotic time that was! Big bodies hurling through space willy-nilly, banging into each other like bumper cars! But no worries. I brought them all in line!

Mercury

I may be smallest, but I'm closest to Sun. So it's easy to get burned on my hot surface. Even the spacecraft sent up to orbit me need special heat shields. I'm rocky, like the other inner, terrestrial planets, and I'm pocked with lots of craters. Why? Because my atmosphere is so thin, meteors don't burn up before they crash into me.

Venus

I'm also a rocky, terrestrial planet. I spin really slowly, in the opposite direction from most other planets. I'm blanketed with a thick atmosphere of greenhouse gases and clouds made of sulfuric acid. The gases trap Sun's heat, making me the hottest planet in the solar system. *Youch!* I'm a scorcher!

Earth

I'm the biggest of the terrestrial planets, and I have a very active surface because my crust and upper mantle are made of huge plates that are constantly on the move. That creates lots of volcanoes, mountains, and canyons! My atmosphere keeps me warm so a lot of my water stays liquid, like my oceans—which are where life began! I'm the only planet in the solar system known to have life.

Mars

I'm another terrestrial planet, rocky and small, but I'm cold since I'm farther from Sun. *Brrrr!* Some call me the Red Planet because of the rusty iron minerals that color my soil. My surface shows evidence of ancient floods. Did I ever support life? Good question! I have the biggest volcano in the whole solar system, Olympus Mons. Maybe it's dead, or maybe it's dormant. But if it blows? Watch out!

Jupiter

I'm the biggest planet, the first of the gas giants, the group of planets farther from Sun. I'm a massive ball of hydrogen and helium, which means my surface isn't solid. So don't try to land on me! I'm also stormy. One of my storms, the Great Red Spot, is larger than Earth and has been raging for at least 150 years. And *pssst!* Don't let Saturn tell you he's the only one with rings. I've got rings, too. Mine are just harder to see.

Saturn

I'm also a gas giant made of swirling hydrogen and helium. My rings are spectacular. They're made of chunks of ice and rock, some as tiny as grains of sand, some as large as houses. The pieces are probably bits of comets and asteroids and even moons that were shattered by asteroids or torn apart by my forceful gravity. True, the other gas and ice giants all have rings, too, but theirs are faint, and people on Earth can see mine using only a simple telescope.

Uranus

I'm an ice giant made of water, methane gas, and ammonia fluids. That's a lot of icy, flowing materials swirling above my core. My atmosphere is mostly hydrogen and helium, but there's also a small amount of methane, and it makes me look blue-green. Like Venus, I rotate in the opposite direction of the other planets. But I rotate on my side—nice trick!—the only planet to do so.

Neptune

I'm the last planet in the solar system. Since I'm farthest from Sun, it takes me a long time to complete a single orbit. One of my years is 165 Earth years! I'm an ice giant made of water, ammonia, and methane over a small, rocky core. Like my nearest pal, Uranus, I have a touch of methane in my atmosphere, so I look blue, too. But my blue's even brighter, so there's probably some other unknown chemical in the mix. And hold on to your hats. *Whoosh!* I'm the windiest planet, with winds many times stronger than Earth's hurricanes.

To Mom, our family's bright star, and to Phoebe, our youngest planet
—J.C.

To Gillian MacKenzie, a true superstar
—J.M.

Library of Congress Cataloging-in-Publication Data
Names: Carr, Jan (M. J.), author. | Medina, Juana, illustrator.
Title: Star of the party: the solar system celebrates! / written by Jan Carr; illustrated by Juana Medina.
Description: First edition. | New York: Crown Books for Young Readers, [2021] | Audience: Ages 4–8. | Audience: Grades K–1. |
Summary: All the planets in the solar system decide to throw Sun a birthday party. Includes facts about the planets.
Identifiers: LCCN 2020020514 (print) | LCCN 2020020515 (ebook) | ISBN 978-1-5247-7312-0 (hardcover) |
ISBN 978-1-5247-7313-7 (library binding) | ISBN 978-1-5247-7315-1 (trade paperback) | ISBN 978-1-5247-7314-4 (ebook)
Subjects: CYAC: Planets—Fiction. | Sun—Fiction. | Birthdays—Fiction. | Parties—Fiction.
Classification: LCC PZ7.C22947 St 2021 (print) | LCC PZ7.C22947 (ebook) | DDC [E]—dc23

Book design by Nicole de las Heras

MANUFACTURED IN CHINA
10 9 8 7 6 5 4 3 2 1
First Edition

STAR OF THE PARTY

The Solar System Celebrates!

Written by

Jan Carr

Illustrated by

Juana Medina

Crown Books for Young Readers ♔ New York

O
NE DAY THE PLANETS GOT TO TALKING. As usual,
the conversation revolved around the sun.
"Sun sure is looking bright today," Neptune said proudly.
"Really bright," said Uranus. "For a star that's 4.6 billion years old."

Whoa, 4.6 billion? That's a lot of birthdays!

"Hey!" said Earth. "We should have a *birthday* party!"

The other planets burst out laughing. Earth always wanted to do things *people* liked to do.

"How many people do you have living on you now, anyway, Earth?" asked Mars.

"Somewhere over seven billion," she said. "Going on eight."

"Now *that's* a lot of birthdays!" said Mars.

"Let's plan Sun's party!" said Jupiter.
"We'll invite a lot of stars."
"No," said Earth. "No other stars."
"Why not?"

"Because *Sun* is our star. We'll keep it cozy—only those of us who love Sun best. Just our solar system."

Mercury started a guest list.

"Pluto," he wrote. Mercury particularly liked Pluto. Pluto was the only planet smaller than he was.

"Pluto?" said Jupiter. "Pluto's not a planet! Don't you read the news? He was recategorized in 2006! He's a *dwarf planet*. Way too little to be in our club!"

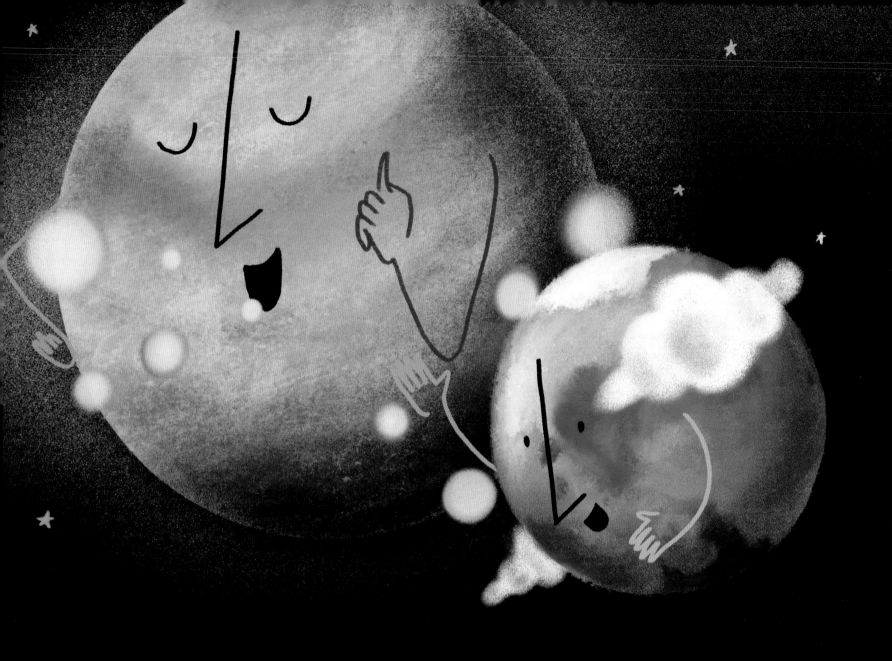

Hotshot Jupiter! What a know-it-all! So big and bulky. And always bragging about his size. Mercury sulked. Did this mean *he* was the smallest now?

"Don't worry," said Earth. "We can invite Pluto. But we'll group him with other dwarf planets."

"Ha!" laughed Jupiter. "At the kids' table!"

Neither did Venus. Which was kind of funny, because Venus was, well, *moony*.

"A space case!" said Saturn. "An oddball! She rotates in the wrong direction!"

Wrong? No. It was just different! Venus spun in the opposite direction from most of the other planets. But Uranus did, too.

"Venus and I were in a few collisions early on," said Uranus. "And something big must've slammed into her. It could've knocked her upside down, or sent her spinning in the other direction."

"Maybe," said Venus. "But some people think Sun's responsible."

"Sun?"

"Sun's gravity. It could've tugged on the thick gases that envelop me, creating tides in my atmosphere. They might've pulled me in the opposite direction. Nobody knows for sure. It's a mystery!"

"What's next on our to-do list?"
asked Neptune.
  "Place cards," said Earth. "They tell
us where to sit."

"No!" cried Mercury. Mercury liked his position. He was closest to Sun.

"But place cards are fun," said Earth. "We can decorate them!"

"Oh, well, in that case!" Mercury volunteered for the job. He wanted to draw Jupiter with a really ridiculous mustache.

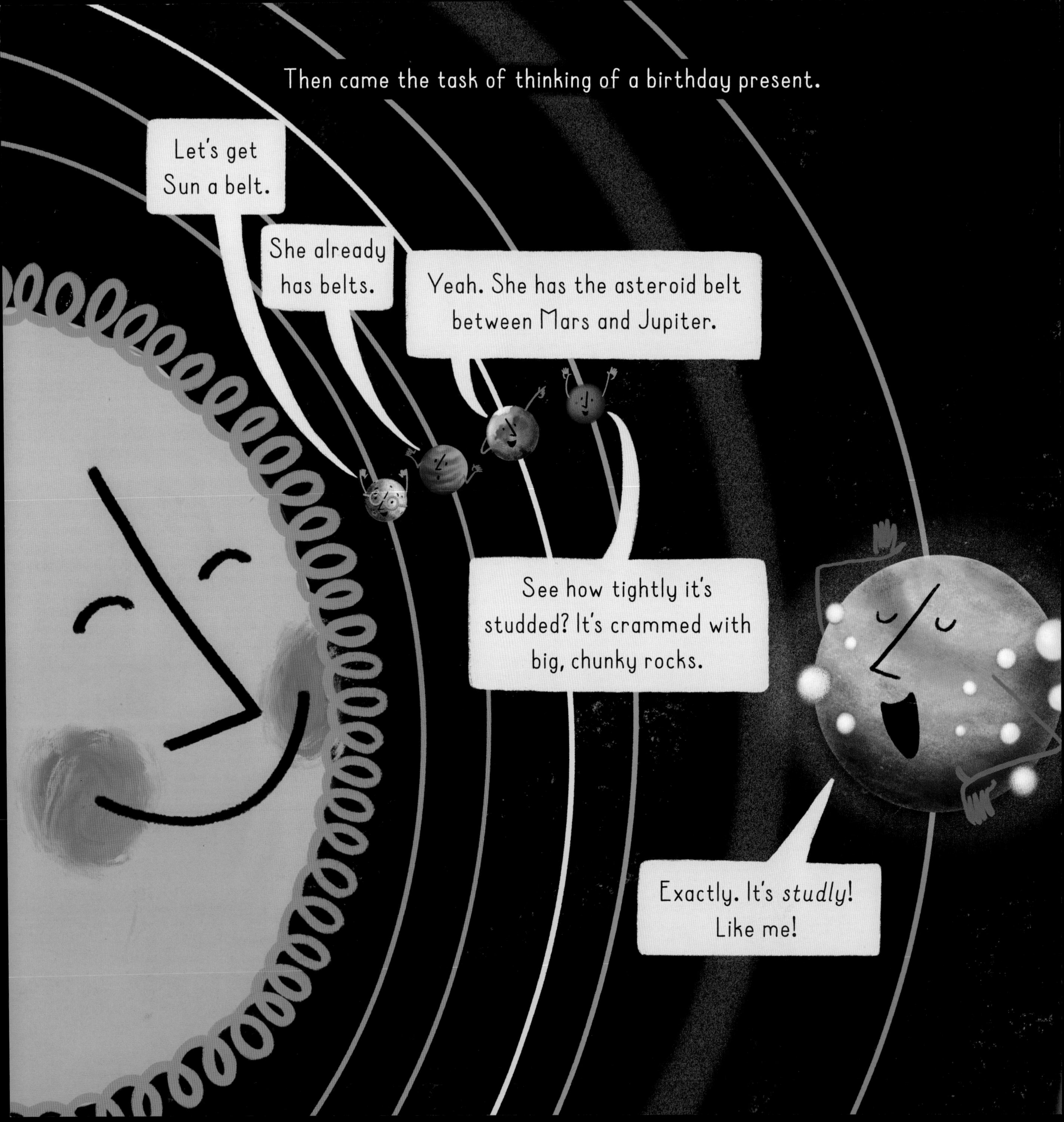
Then came the task of thinking of a birthday present.
Let's get Sun a belt.
She already has belts.
Yeah. She has the asteroid belt between Mars and Jupiter.
See how tightly it's studded? It's crammed with big, chunky rocks.
Exactly. It's *studly*! Like me!

All the planets wanted to look snazzy for the celebration. Saturn was strutting, flouncing his rings and ringlets.

"Places, everyone! Time to party down!"

To start the festivities, the solar system put on a show.

Meteors showered the sky. And a comet streaked past. Fireworks!

An asteroid whizzed through, crashing the party.

And just then, by total coincidence, some people on Earth, who had no idea that the planets were in the middle of a big celebration, sent up a rocket.

"Oh no," said Mars, Earth's next-door neighbor. "They're not sending up another Mars rover, are they? Enough with the exploration! Can't a planet have any privacy?"

Soon it was time for the testimonials. Each of the planets went in order.

I'm so glad we're close, Sun.

Twinkle, twinkle, glittery star,
Do I wonder who you are?
Did your pull make me go flip-flop?
I know in my heart you're tip-top.

All on Earth salute you! Animals bask in your warmth. Plants tilt their faces toward you. And people wish on a lucky star. That's YOU!

We go back a long way, Sun.
Back to the time of my ancient floods.
Did I ever support life? *Shhh!*
That's our little secret.

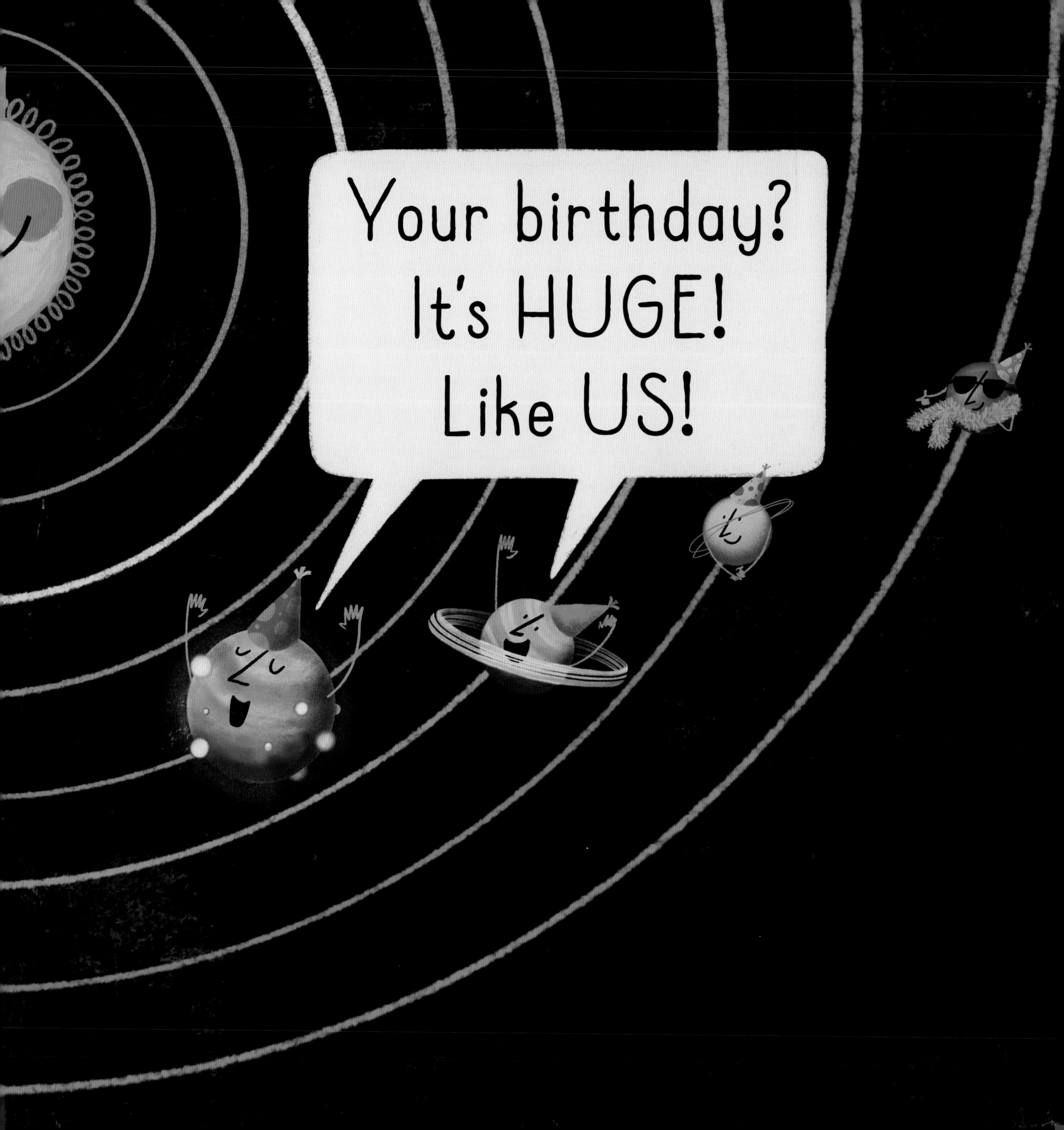
Your birthday? It's HUGE! Like US!

Suddenly, there was another voice. Or was there? It was faint. "Hello, Sun," it said. Where was the voice coming from? "I'm in your orbit, too."

Whoa! A mysterious stranger!

"Who are you?" asked Neptune.

"Some call me Planet X," said the
voice. "But you can call me Planet Nine."

"Okay," said Neptune. "But *where* are you?"
"Far in the outer reaches of your solar system. Some think I used to
be closer, but got flung out long ago."
"Wow," said Venus. "Do you actually exist?"
"Maybe," said the voice. "Or maybe not. Do *you*?"
"Sheesh!" said Venus. "Don't get all spacey on me!"
But then, just like that, the voice disappeared. *Poof!* It was gone.
A shiver ran through the planets. Had the voice been real? Or had they
somehow dreamed it?

The planets stared out beyond the cozy circle of their solar system. There were so many stars in the distance, winking and blinking—billions and billions. Did all those stars have planets, too? The universe was vast.

"Cosmic," said Venus.

Suddenly, there was a rumble. A volcano erupted, shooting up high. Kind of like a burp. Or a fart. Wouldn't you know. It was on Io, one of Jupiter's moons. Her volcanoes were always spewing forth.

Oops! Excuse me. Too much partying!

All the planets looked at Sun. Had she had a good time? Had she liked her party?

They waited, hushed, with no chatter other than the fizz and spit and sputter of the universe.

Sun was a star of few words. . . .

"Stellar!" she cried.
She was beaming! Radiant!
The party was a glowing success.

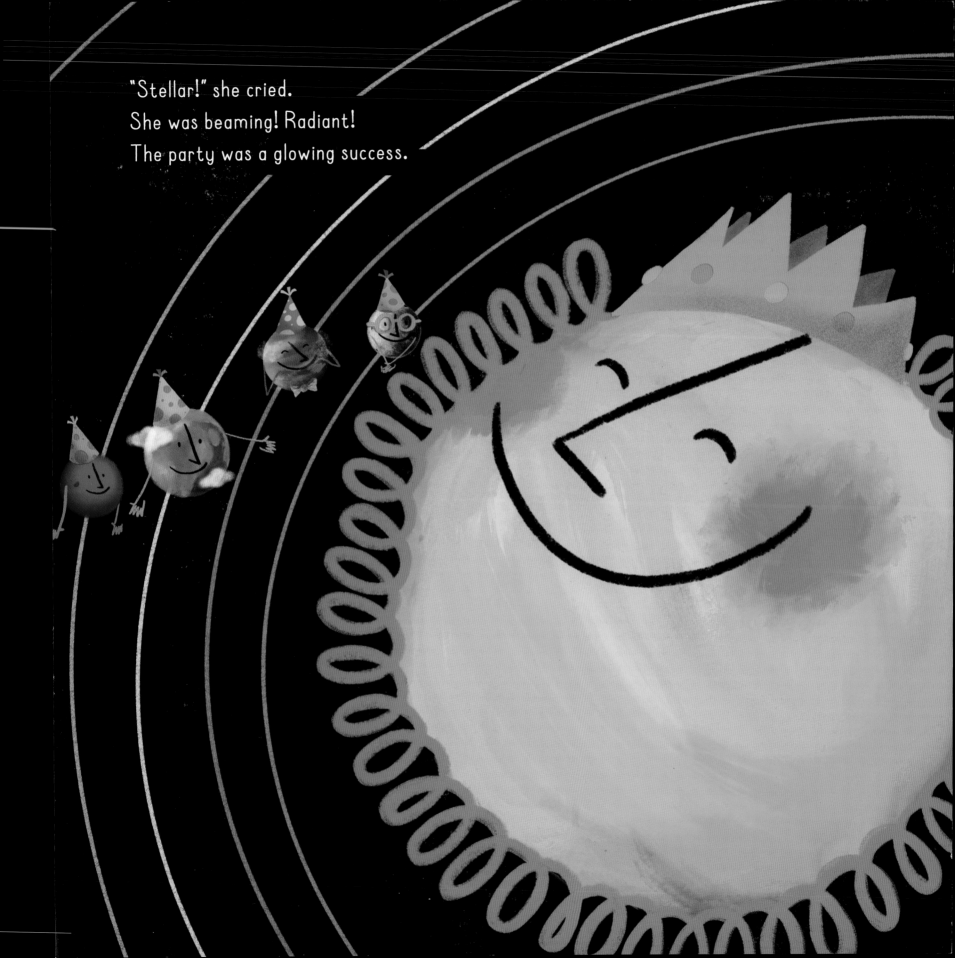

BREAKING NEWS! CHANGE IS COMING!

Since astronomers are always learning more about our solar system, some of the information in this book may change. For the latest updates, please visit these reputable websites:

Smithsonian National Air and Space Museum:
airandspace.si.edu/exhibitions/exploring-the-planets/online/

American Museum of Natural History:
amnh.org/exhibitions/permanent/the-universe/planets

NASA Kids' Club: nasa.gov/kidsclub/index.html

NASA Science Space Place: spaceplace.nasa.gov

NASA Science Solar System Exploration:
solarsystem.nasa.gov/solar-system/our-solar-system/overview/

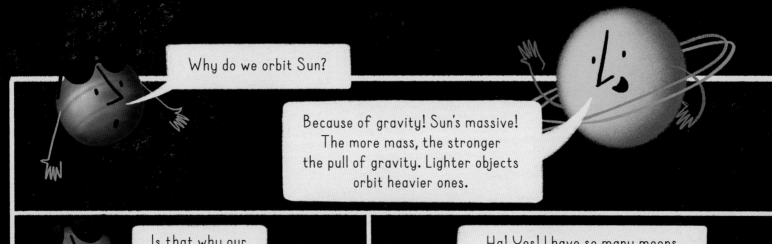

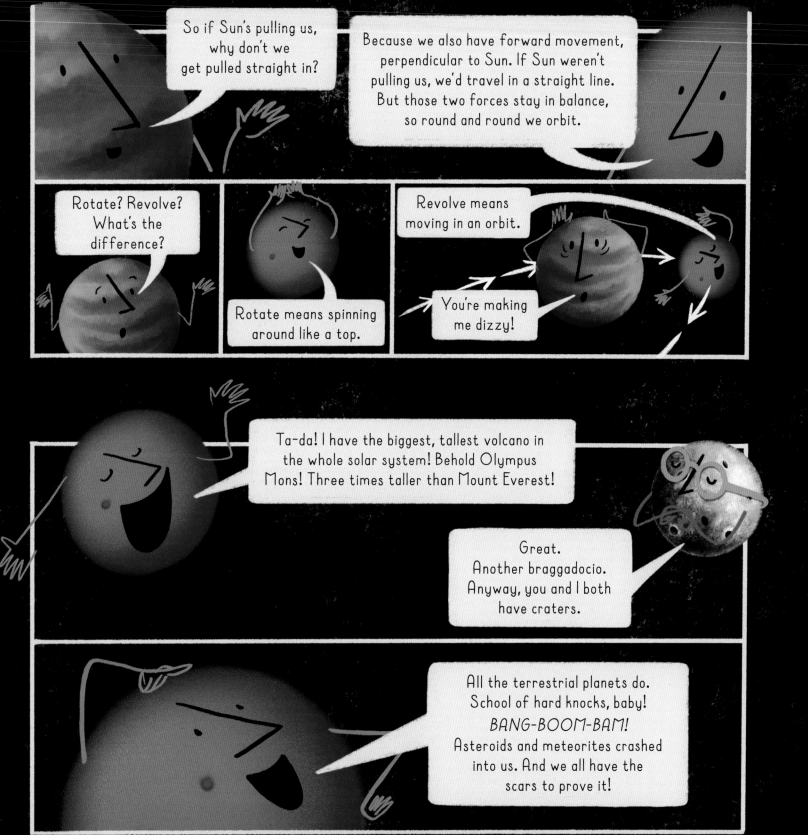

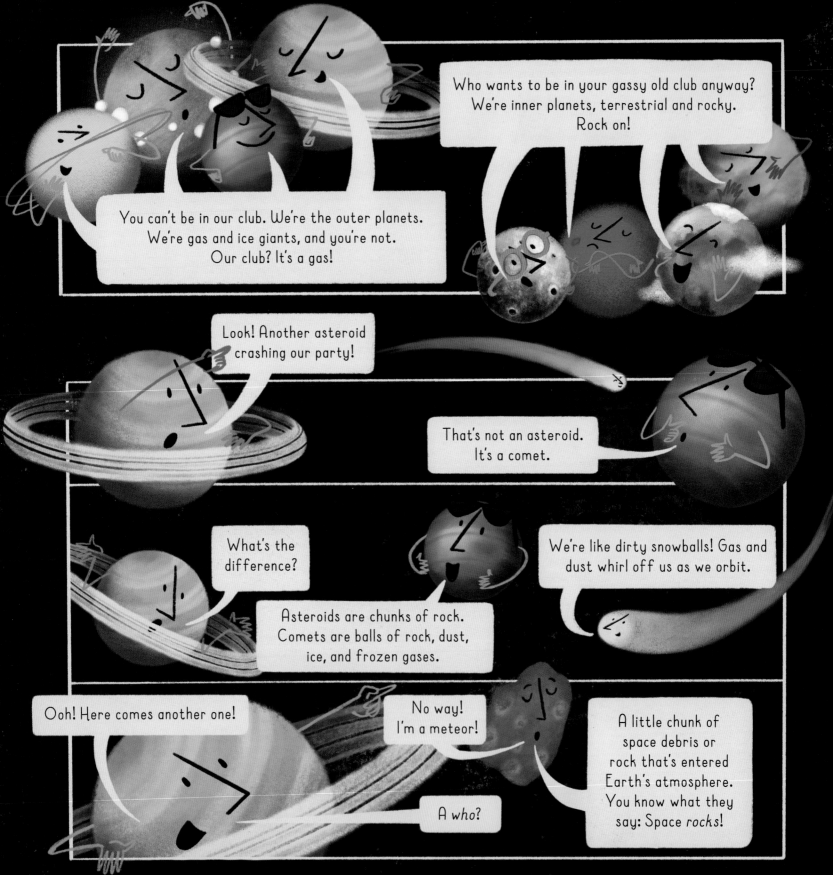